ELOISE WILKIN
Stories

A GOLDEN BOOK • NEW YORK

The material contained in this book was taken from the following Golden Book publications:
Busy Timmy copyright © 1948 by Random House, Inc.
Guess Who Lives Here copyright © 1949 by Random House, Inc.
My Little Golden Book About God copyright © 1956, 1975 by Random House, Inc.
Wonders of Nature copyright © 1957 by Random House, Inc.
A Child's Garden of Verses copyright © 1957 by Random House, Inc.
We Help Mommy copyright © 1959 by Random House, Inc.
Baby Listens copyright © 1960 by Random House, Inc.
Baby Dear copyright © 1962 by Random House, Inc.
Baby Looks copyright © 1960 by Random House, Inc.
Baby's Mother Goose copyright © 1958 by Random House, Inc.
Eloise Wilkin's Book of Poems copyright © 1988 by Deborah Springett. Illustrations copyright © 1988 by Eloise Wilkin.
A Remembrance of Eloise Wilkin copyright © 1987 by Jane Werner Watson.
Library of Congress Control Number: 2004096079
ISBN: 0-375-82928-8
www.goldenbooks.com
www.randomhouse.com/kids
Book design by Roberta Ludlow
PRINTED IN CHINA   First Random House Edition 2005
13 14 15 16 17 18 19 20

Contents

Introduction

By Deborah Wilkin Springett

The award-winning artist Eloise Wilkin is best known as an illustrator of Little Golden Books. Millions of readers have regarded with wonder and delight her renderings of adorable babies, winsome children, and cuddly animals in old-fashioned settings and delicately crafted landscapes. But despite her many achievements, my mother was incredibly modest about her work. The main focus of her life was her family. Consequently, we as children did not fully appreciate her remarkable talent. To Ann, Sidney, Jeremy, and me, Eloise Wilkin was first and foremost our mother.

Eloise Margaret Burns was born on March 30, 1904, in Rochester, New York. She was the third of four children and liked to describe herself as the rebel in the family. When Eloise was two years old, the Burnses moved to New York City. Every year the four siblings would spend the summer with their relatives in western New York State. Their father, Robert Burns, would help them board the train at Grand Central Station and send advance notice of their arrival in a telegram stating, "Burns Comedy Four arriving at port."

My mother once told me that as a child she was fascinated with bugs and would spend hours during the summer observing them. But during those holidays, Eloise would become terribly homesick. With a lump in her throat, she would stand on her grandparents' porch gazing at stars twinkling in the night skies. Years later, these recurring themes of nature and childhood memories would find expression in her beautifully illustrated pictures of children.

Eloise's family was startled when, at age eleven, she won a drawing contest for New York schoolchildren. It was because of this award that Eloise's parents decided to send her to art school. In 1923, she completed her training in fine and applied arts at the Rochester Athenaeum and Mechanics Institute, now the Rochester Institute of Technology. After graduation, Eloise and Joan Esley, a close friend and former classmate, opened an art studio in Rochester. It was a constant struggle for the two young artists to obtain work, so they eventually decided to move to New York City, where they hoped to find a more lucrative job market. A week after their arrival, Eloise walked into the offices of the Century Company and was given her first book to illustrate, *The Shining Hours*.

After four years, Eloise's budding career as an artist was put on hold when she married Sidney Wilkin on August 19, 1930. For the next decade, my mother set aside her paintbrushes and devoted her time and energy to raising four children.

After this long hiatus from her artwork, it was difficult for Eloise to resume her illustrating career. My mother felt she had lost her ability to draw. But once she returned to the daily discipline of being a working artist, Eloise regained her confidence. This process began when her sister, Esther, wrote a book called *Mrs. Peregrine and the Yak* and submitted it to the Julia Elsworth Ford Foundation Contest. She asked Eloise to illustrate the book, which was chosen for publication by the Henry Holt Company. This was the first successful collaboration between the two sisters. Many more were to follow.

In 1944, Eloise signed an exclusive contract with Simon and Schuster, the original publisher of Little Golden Books, to illustrate three Little Golden Books a year. This association was to last for several years. With each succeeding book she illustrated, Eloise added a new dimension to her artistic style. And when the Polaroid Land Camera was invented, Eloise found it useful in taking pictures of live models. Her grandchildren were delighted and flattered when she asked them to pose for one of her Little Golden Books.

To this day, Eloise Wilkin remains one of the most collectible of all the Golden Book illustrators.

The field of doll design was also included in Eloise Wilkin's creative abilities. For twenty years, she worked to produce a doll that was soft and cuddly and resembled a newborn baby. My mother was a perfectionist. I can remember a trail of clay embedded in furniture and carpets as she struggled to perfect a model she considered suitable to market. In 1960, Vogue Dolls, Inc., launched Baby Dear, the first doll designed by Eloise Wilkin. Baby Dear caused a sensation in the doll industry. Millions were sold. In 1960 Nikita Khrushchev came to New York City to deliver his famous shoe-thumping speech at the United Nations. When he and his Russian delegation saw Eloise's doll in the window of FAO Schwarz, they purchased thirteen Baby Dears to take back to Russia. Eventually Eloise would design a total of eight dolls for Vogue and the Madame Alexander Doll Company. *Baby Dear* and *So Big* were Little Golden Books written by Esther Wilkin, and illustrated by Eloise Wilkin, that featured two of my mother's doll designs.

Eloise Wilkin believed that an artist's creativity sprang from the very depths of her being. Her warmth and sensitivity, her faith and spiritual nature, and her love for all living things became integral parts of every page she illustrated. When she died on October 4, 1987, the world lost a beloved illustrator and doll designer. Our family lost not only a mother and a grand-mother but also the most extraordinarily gifted woman we have ever known.

—*Deborah Wilkin Springett*
December 2003

BUSY TIMMY

Eloise Wilkin

Timmy is
a big boy.

He can put on his outdoor clothes.

He can find his shovel
and his big sand pail.

He goes down the steps.
No one has to help him.
He's a big boy now.

He climbs in his sand-box.

A robin sees Timmy and comes flying.

A squirrel sees Timmy and comes running.

A rabbit sees Timmy and comes hopping.
They all watch Timmy make little holes and
big hills.

He rides on his horse all
around the flower bed,

up bumps and down bumps

and back home again.

Timmy goes up the steps

and opens the door all by himself.

He gets ready for his bath.
No one has to help him.
He's a big boy now.

He splashes in the bathtub,
and sails his new boat.

He puts on his own bib,

and holds his own cup.

He eats all his supper with no help at all.

He brushes his own teeth.

He climbs into bed, all by himself!

"Hush!" says the robin.

"Hush!" says the squirrel.

"Shush!" says the rabbit.
"Timmy is a big boy, and Timmy
is going to sleep!"

Yes,
Timmy *is* a big boy—
and he is sound asleep.

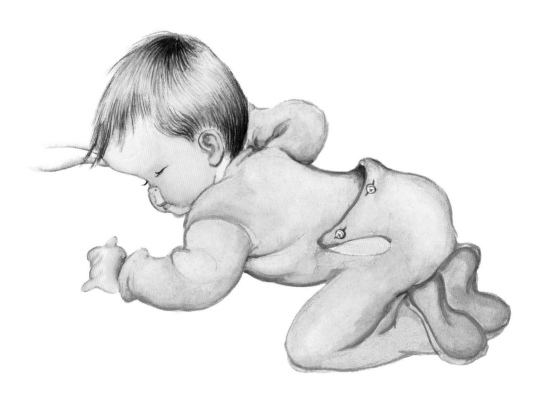

You are big, too.
Timmy does a lot of things. So can you!

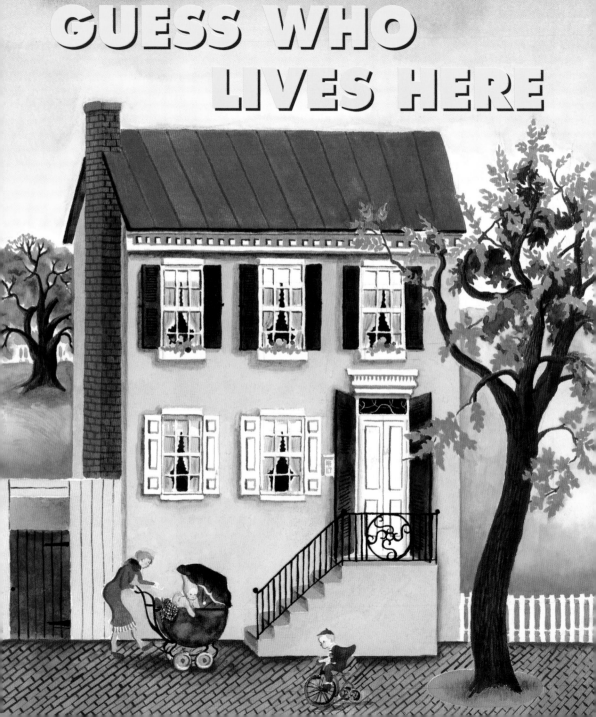

Somebody lives in this house.
He wears green overalls
And a striped sweater.

He likes to ride a bike
And build with blocks.

Guess who it is!

It's Terry.

Somebody lives in this house.
She has curly hair and she smiles very often.
She wears a dress and sometimes
 an apron.
She cooks good things to eat
 every night,
And she tucks Terry into bed
 with a kiss.

Guess who it is!

It's Terry's mother.

Somebody else lives in this house.

He is very tall,

And he walks with long steps.

He goes out to work in the morning,

And sometimes he brings Terry a present

when he comes home at night.

Guess who it is!

It's Terry's father.

Somebody else lives in this house.
She is very short.
She can't stand up even holding on to a chair.
She takes her milk out of a bottle.
She has only three teeth.

Guess who it is!

It's Terry's baby sister.

Somebody else lives in this house.
He has rough brown hair
And a tail he can wag.
All he can say is "Bow-wow!"
    or "Woof-woof!"
He loves to go everywhere Terry goes.

Guess who it is!

It's Terry's dog Wolfie.

Somebody else lives in this house.
She is soft and furry.
She has claws that can scratch, but she doesn't
    scratch very often.
She drinks milk from a saucer on the floor.
She likes to sleep in nice warm places.

Guess who it is!

It's Terry's cat Silkie.

Somebody else lives in this house.
He is very very tiny
And can run very fast.
He is gray all over and his tail's
      like a little sharp spike.
He comes out at night to hunt for crumbs.

Guess who it is!

It's the mouse in Terry's cellar.

Somebody lives in the big tree beside this house.
She lives in a nest that she built on a branch.
She has four blue eggs in that nest.
She sits on the nest to keep the eggs warm,
Because her babies are inside them.

Guess who it is!

It's a mother robin.

Somebody else lives in the tree by the house.
He has long gray fur
And a beautiful wavy tail.
He can jump very far from one branch to another.
He loves to eat nuts in his tiny sharp claws.

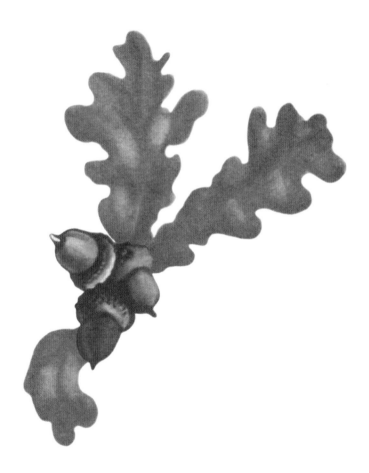

Guess who it is!

It's a squirrel.

Sometimes somebody comes to this house
  before anyone in it is awake.
He doesn't ring the doorbell.
He sets down some bottles on the porch.
He picks up the empty bottles Terry's mother
  has put there.
Then he goes on to
  the house next door.

Guess who it is!

It's the milkman on Terry's street.

Sometimes somebody rings the doorbell
    of this house.
He wears a blue suit.
He carries a big heavy bag on his back.
He takes letters out of his bag,
And puts them in the box beside the
    front door.

Guess who it is!

It's the postman on Terry's street.

Some days something comes down from the sky—
"Patter-pit-patter!" it says on the roof.
"Splashity-splash!" it says on the walk.
The flowers in the window box shine with wetness,
And all the leaves on the big tree drip.

Guess what it is!

It's the rain.

But most days there's something shining down
on this house.
It makes the flowers in the window box grow.
It makes all the people say to each other,

"What a very nice day it is today!"

Guess what it is!

It's the sunshine.

Sometimes something blows round and
    round this house.
It says "Whoo-oo!" in the chimney.
It rattles the windows.
It swings the nest on the branch of the tree.

Guess what it is!

It's the wind.

Sometimes at night something shines
        on this house.
It isn't warm like the sun.
Sometimes it's a thin little silver curve.
Sometimes it looks like half a cookie.
Sometimes it's big and round and shines
        like a mirror.

It shines on the squirrel in his little tree house.

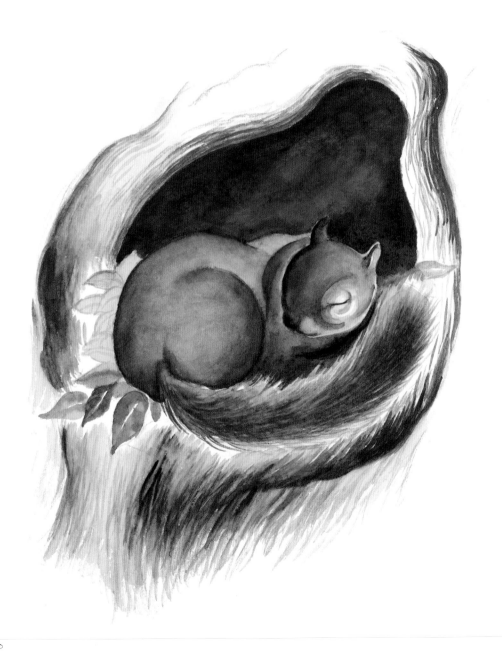

It shines on the robin in her nest on the branch.

It shines on Terry's baby sister in her crib—

And on Terry's father and mother fast asleep.

It shines in the window on the mouse on the floor—

And on Silkie, too sleepy to chase him.

It shines on Terry—

And on Wolfie, stretched out on the floor.

Guess what it is!

It's the moon!

My Little Golden Book About
GOD

GOD IS GREAT.

Look at the stars in the evening sky,
so many millions of miles away
that the light you see shining left its star
long, long years before you were born.

Yet even beyond the farthest star,
God knows the way.
Think of the snow-capped mountain peaks.
Those peaks were crumbling away with
age before the first people lived on earth.
Yet when they were raised up sharp and new
God was there, too.

Bend down to touch the smallest flower.
Watch the busy ant tugging at his load.
See the flash of jewels on the insect's back.
This tiny world your two hands could span,
like the oceans and mountains and far-
    off stars,
God planned.

Think of our earth, spinning in space . . .

so that now, for a day of play and work
we face the sunlight, then we turn away—

to the still, soft darkness for rest and sleep.
This, too, is God's doing.

For GOD IS GOOD.

God gives us everything we need—
shelter from cold and wind and rain,
clothes to wear and food to eat.

God gives us flowers, the songs of birds,
the laughter of brooks, the deep song of the sea.

He sends the sunshine

to make things grow,

sends in its turn
the needed rain.

81

God makes us grow, too, with minds and eyes
to look about our wonderful world,
to see its beauty, to feel its might.

He gives us a small, still voice in our hearts
to help us tell wrong from right.
God gives us hopes and wishes and dreams,
plans for our grown-up years ahead.

He gives us memories of yesterdays,
so that happy times and people we love
we can keep with us always in our hearts.
For GOD IS LOVE.

God is the love of our mother's kiss,

the warm, strong hug of our daddy's arms.

God is in all the love we feel
for playmates and family and friends.

When we're hurt or sorry or lonely or sad,
if we think of God, He is with us there.

God whispers to us in our hearts:
"Do not fear, I am here,
And I love you, my dear.
Close your eyes and sleep tight,
For tomorrow will be bright.
All is well, dear child.
Good night."

WONDERS
OF NATURE

Isn't it a wonder
the way the woods know
that spring is coming
before the snow is gone?

The sleeping plants
send up green shoots.
And the tree buds
swell and burst.

Isn't it a wonder
that some seeds
have wings . . .

ASH

ELM

MAPLE

MILKWEED

and some have
tiny silken
parachutes,

DANDELION

and some seeds
are hidden away
in fruits . . .

APPLE

CORN

BEAN

BEAN

and that every seed,
no matter how tiny,
has a whole tiny plant
inside, with food to use
when it starts to grow?

95

Isn't it a wonder
that under the sea
there are beautiful,
strange gardens
where the "flowers" are
animals?

SEA GRAPES

SEA ANEMONE

SEA LILY

SEA CUCUMBER

SEA URCHIN

SEA ANEMONE

Sea anemones, sea lilies,
sea cucumbers, and sea grapes—
all are animals!

SEA CUCUMBER

SEA ANEMONE

Isn't it a wonder
that tiny coral animals
under the sea,
which never move,
build great towers
and whole islands
of their tiny shells?

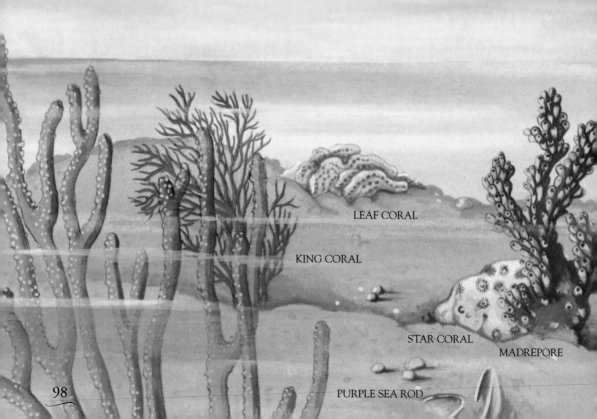

LEAF CORAL

KING CORAL

STAR CORAL

MADREPORE

PURPLE SEA ROD

ORGAN-PIPE
CORAL

BRAIN CORAL

CUP CORAL

Isn't it a wonder
that on the dry desert
some plants have thick stems
in which they store water . . .
and no leaves at all . . .
and lots of prickly spines
to keep thirsty animals
from eating them up?

And the kangaroo rat
who lives on the desert
never drinks water,
but makes it in his body
out of crisp, dry seeds.

Isn't it a wonder
that the beaver
can bite a young tree through
in just a few minutes?

He bites off the branches and uses them
to build a dam across a stream.

And all the birds around,
and the squirrels and opossums,
the deer and the moose,
enjoy that beaver pond.

Isn't it a wonder
that in the jungles
the leaves grow so thickly
overhead that some birds and
animals on the ground
never see the sun?

And there are insects
that look just
like leaves?

And trees start growing
high in the air
on top of other trees,
and send spindly roots down
to the ground?

Isn't it a wonder
that far up north
in the land of ice and snow
we call the arctic,

animals have winter coats
of fur as white as the snow?

Isn't it a wonder that some birds fly
thousands of miles over ocean and land . . .

and return to the same special spots,
to lay their eggs?

That salmon swim
hundreds of miles to shore
and far up the rivers
and over the waterfalls . . .

to return to the same special spots
to lay their eggs?

Isn't it a wonder
that fireflies
have lights in their bodies
they can flash on and off . . .

that crickets "chirp" by rubbing
their wings?

That some fish
deep in the ocean
have little "electric lights"
dangling in front
of their noses as they swim?

LANTERNFISH

ANGLER

Or little lights
along their sides?

FIREFLY FISH

Isn't it a wonder
that out in the pond
smooth wiggly tadpoles
lose their tails
and grow legs,
and turn into frogs?

And that fuzzy caterpillars
weave silken cocoons
around themselves
and go to sleep,
then wake up as pretty moths
or butterflies?

113

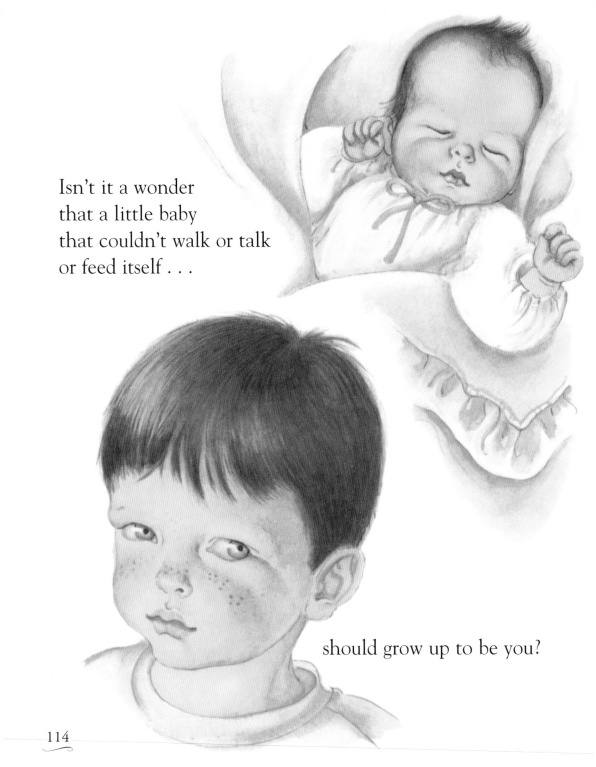

Isn't it a wonder
that a little baby
that couldn't walk or talk
or feed itself . . .

should grow up to be you?

Rain

The rain is raining all around,
It falls on field and tree,
It rains on the umbrellas here,
And on the ships at sea.

The Swing

How do you like to go up in a swing,
  Up in the air so blue?
Oh, I do think it the pleasantest thing
  Ever a child can do!

Up in the air and over the wall,
  Till I can see so wide,
Rivers and trees and cattle and all
  Over the countryside—

Till I look down on the garden green,
  Down on the roof so brown—
Up in the air I go flying again,
  Up in the air and down!

From A Child's Garden of Verses by Robert Louis Stevenson

From A Child's Garden of Verses *by Robert Louis Stevenson*

Windy Nights

Whenever the moon and stars are set,
    Whenever the wind is high,
All night long in the dark and wet,
    A man goes riding by.
Late in the night when the fires are out,
Why does he gallop and gallop about?

Whenever the trees are crying aloud,
    And ships are tossed at sea,
By, on the highway, low and loud,
    By at the gallop goes he.
By at the gallop he goes, and then
By he comes back at the gallop again.

We Help Mommy

We help Mommy every day.
We help her in the morning, as soon as we get up.
We take off our pajamas.

Bobby puts on his pants,
and socks, and shoes.
He can dress himself.
I put on mine.
Over my head goes
my shirt.
Oops! My arm is stuck.
Mommy will help me
pull it out.

Mommy buckles
my shoes.
"You're a good girl,
Martha," says
Mommy.
"You can almost
dress yourself."

We all go down for breakfast.
Bobby breaks the eggs for Daddy to fry.
I put bread in the toaster.
Out it pops, hot and brown!
"You two are a big help," says Daddy.

We wave good-by to Daddy from the door.
Then it's time to make Mommy's bed.
"Pull the sheet tight," Mommy says.
We pull until there's not a wrinkle left.
"Thank you," says Mommy when we're done.

Swish! swish! goes the broom.
Pfuff! pfuff! goes the dust mop.
Brr! brr! goes the carpet sweeper
as it picks up the dirt.

We are cleaning house.
Under the beds, over the rugs,
in all the corners we clean.
"Here is a dustcloth for you," says Mommy.
Bobby dusts the table-tops
while I mop under the chairs.

Now it's time to wash.
We collect the clothes.
Bobby puts Daddy's clothes
  in the washing machine.
I put my dolly's clothes in.

In goes the soap.
Bang! goes the door.
Hmmmmm! goes the machine.
Round and round the clothes go.
I can see my face in the shiny glass.

127

My clothesline isn't high like Mommy's.
It is just right for me.
I hang up dolly's clothes.
Two clothespins for her dress.
One clothespin for each sock.
And one clothespin for her hat.

We see Ann and Jerry playing in their
sandbox next door.
"Come on over, Martha and Bobby!" they call.
"Run along," says Mommy.
"Take your pails and shovels.
Have fun!"

Once a week we go to the supermarket.
I ride in the cart while Bobby pushes.
Up and down the aisles we go.
"What would you like today?" asks Mommy.

We tell her cereal and apples
and cookies and raisins and a picture book.
We pile them on the counter.
Mommy has two big bags
and Bobby and I have little bags to carry home.

We like to put things away for Mommy.
The cereal goes in the cabinet,
the apples in the basket,
the cookies and raisins on the shelf.
"You're a big help," says Mommy.

Soon it is time for lunch.
Mommy gets the bread and cheese and meat.
I spread butter on two slices.
Bobby puts meat and cheese on two others.
Slap! Mommy puts them together.
What yummy sandwiches!

Now we set the table.

A place mat for Mommy.
And place mats for Bobby and me.
A knife and fork for Mommy.
A fork for each of us.
Napkins for us all.

After lunch Mommy washes the dishes.
She lets me dry the forks and spoons.
"Here's a spoon for you, Martha."
I take it from the dish rack
and rub it all over gently.
Bobby puts the dishes away.

I sit on a stool when I help Mommy bake pies.
Mommy mixes the dough in a big bowl.
She gives me a little ball of dough
to make a treat for Daddy.
Roll, pat. Roll, pat.
I'm making a treat for Daddy.
It's a funny man, with two cherries for eyes,
and one cherry for a mouth.
"Daddy will be very pleased," says Mommy.
And she puts it in the oven.

We've had a busy day helping Mommy.
Soon it is time to put away our toys
and books and clothes and get ready for bed.
Daddy comes to say good-night and tuck me in.
"That was a delicious treat, Martha," he says.
"Thank you for being such a big help to Mommy
and me. Sleep tight."

Baby
Listens

Oh, what are the sounds that Baby hears
When he listens hard with his little ears?

TICK TOCK TICK TOCK
That's the sound of Baby's clock.

GURGLE GURGLE GLUB GLUB
Water's going from Baby's tub.

BUMPETY BUMPETY down the stair—
there goes Baby's teddy bear.

TUM TUM TUM DEE DUM
Baby's beating on his drum.

143

CLICKETY CLACK
CLICKETY CLACK
Baby's train
goes round the track.

144

BEEP BEEP BEEP
goes the car on the street.

145

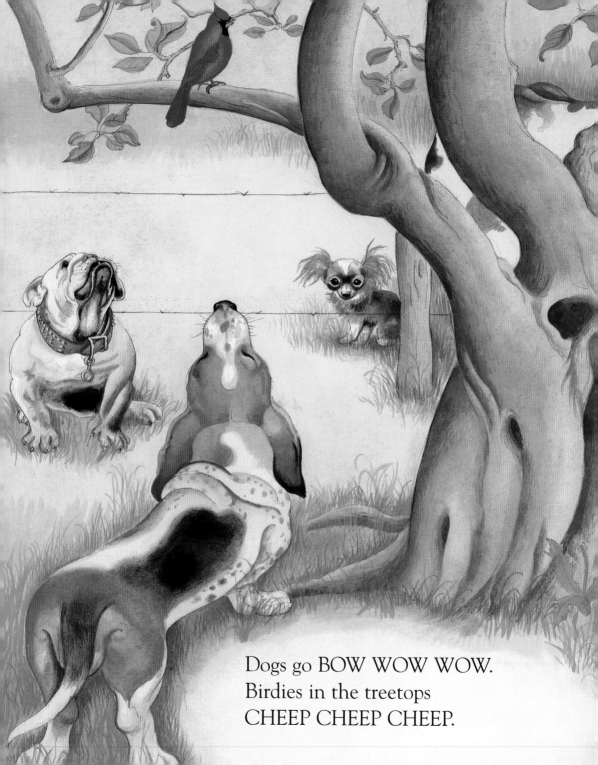

Dogs go BOW WOW WOW.
Birdies in the treetops
CHEEP CHEEP CHEEP.

Pussy cats MEOW
And MOOOOO says the cow.

147

oooOOOOOOOOooo
Screams the siren on the fire truck.
CLANG CLANG CLANG
Goes the bell.

ZOOM ZOOM ZOOM
go the planes
in the sky.
They're way
up high,
you can tell.

BUZZ-Z-Z goes Daddy's razor.

And BUZZ-Z-Z go the bumble bees.

SNAP
goes Mommy's
pocketbook.

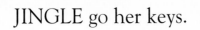

JINGLE go her keys.

Baby rides his kiddie car
SQUEAK
SQUEAK
SQUEAK.

Baby sits and rocks awhile
CREAK CREAK CREAK.

WHIRR-R-R-R goes the beater in the batter.

WHEE-E-E
cries Baby
in his swing.

157

Raindrops PITTER PATTER PATTER.

Bells go
DING DONG
DING.

Oh, these are the sounds that Baby hears
When he listens hard with his little ears!

Baby Dear is my brand-new baby doll.
Daddy brought her to me on a very special day.

It was the day he brought Mommy and our new baby home from the hospital.

Mommy loves her baby.
And I love mine.

We give our babies their bottles.

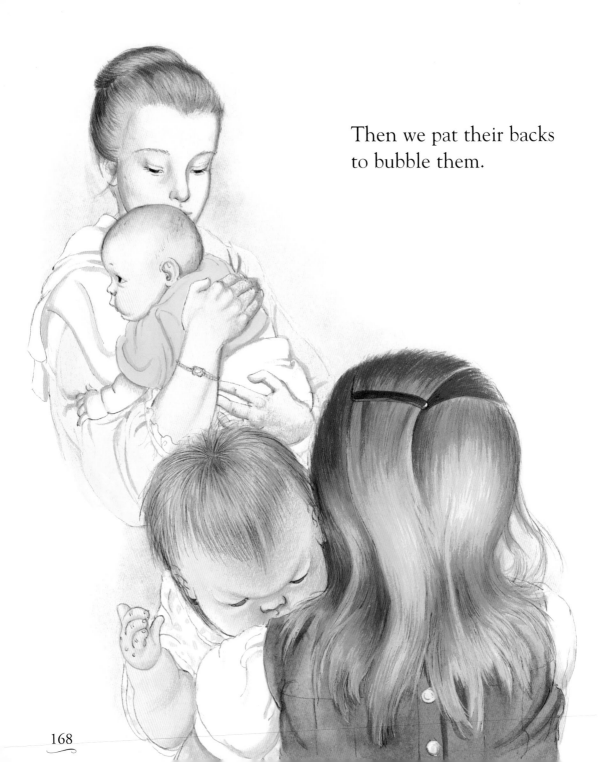

Then we pat their backs
to bubble them.

Mommy changes her baby.

And I change mine.

Mommy bathes her baby. And
I bathe Baby Dear.

We play Little Piggy
with their little pink toes.

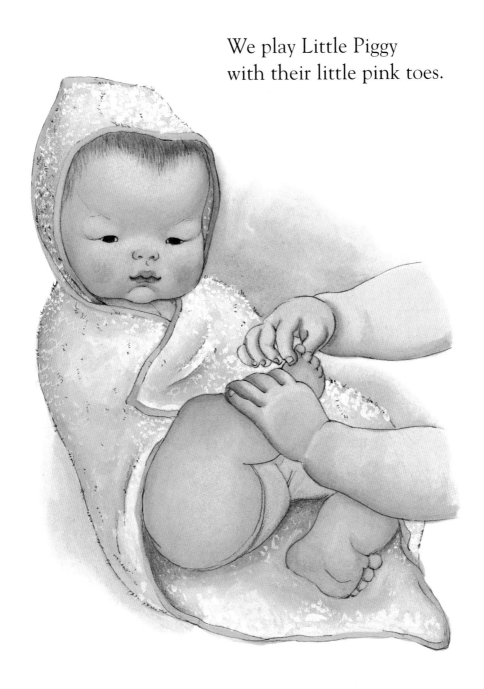

We dress our babies in their bonnets
before we take them out.
   Mommy has a carriage for her baby.
And I have one for Baby Dear.
   We go walking together with our babies.

Mommy's baby sleeps in the little white bed that used to be mine.

My baby sleeps in a cradle all her own.

Mommy has a book
for her baby and I have one
for Baby Dear.

We write things in our books about our babies.

Mommy sings to her baby and I sing to mine.

We smile at our babies and talk to them.
Mommy says this is the way our babies know
they are the most wonderful babies in the world.

Sometimes Mommy lets me hold her baby.
Mommy's baby is my baby sister.

When my baby sister is a big girl
I will let her hold Baby Dear.

Baby Looks

Oh, what are the things that Baby sees
As he creeps around on his hands and knees?

Here is Baby's sock
And here is Baby's shoe.
Baby's lost the laces.
What will Baby do?

See Baby's bonnet
With the pretty blue bow.
See Baby's sweater
With the buttons in a row.

Now Baby's in his stroller,
Ready for a ride.
He's looking all about him,
Eyes open wide.
Look up in the treetop.
What does baby see?
A little birdie singing,
CHEE CHEE CHEE.

Look at Baby's sister
Sliding down the slide.

Now she's in her wagon
Going for a ride.

See Baby's brother
Swinging in the swing

There's Baby's kitty
Playing with a string.

Baby found a little bug
Walking on the ground.
Poked it with his finger,
Didn't make a sound.

Baby found a buttercup,
Found a little clover,
Leaned way down and sniffed them—
Then he tumbled over!

Now the rain is coming down,
It makes the sidewalk shine.
It makes umbrellas all go up
And babies go inside.

See how dark the clouds are,
See the birdies fly,
See the pretty rainbow
'Way up in the sky.

Over there
Is Baby's chair,
His silver cup,
And silver spoon . . .
Baby's supper time
comes soon.

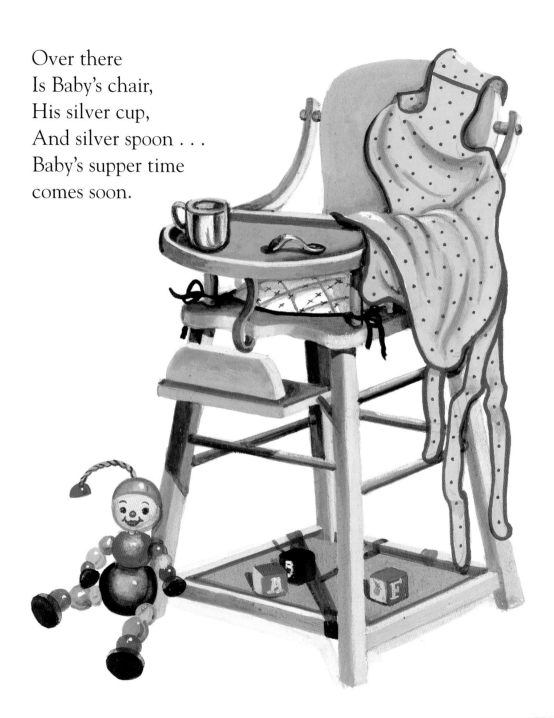

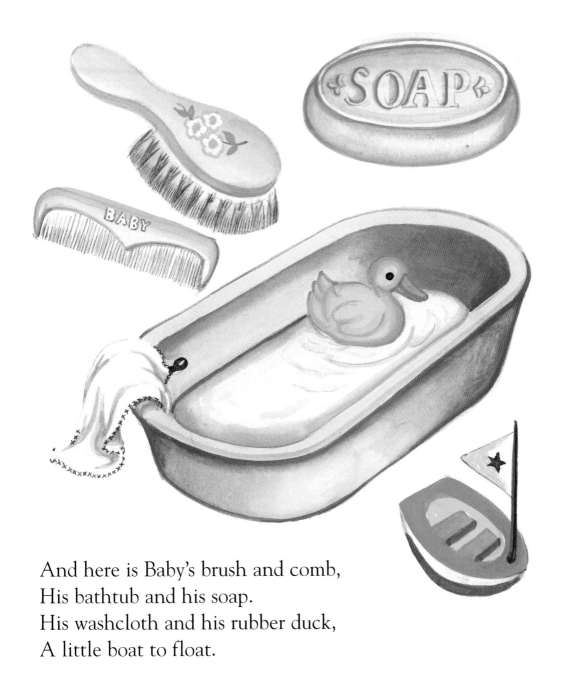

And here is Baby's brush and comb,
His bathtub and his soap.
His washcloth and his rubber duck,
A little boat to float.

Now Baby's in his crib.
Asleep he soon will be,
His blanket and his bear
To keep him company.

202

Looking through the window
Is a big, yellow moon,
Shining on the floor
Where the sun was at noon.
See Baby's shadow
High on the wall.
Sometimes it's short
And sometimes it's tall.
When the light goes out
It isn't there at all.

Oh, this is the world that Baby sees
As he creeps around on his hands and knees.

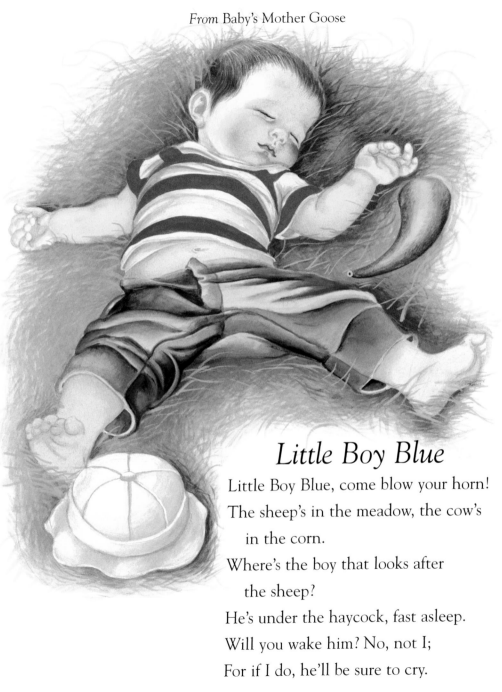

Little Boy Blue

Little Boy Blue, come blow your horn!
The sheep's in the meadow, the cow's
    in the corn.
Where's the boy that looks after
    the sheep?
He's under the haycock, fast asleep.
Will you wake him? No, not I;
For if I do, he'll be sure to cry.

205

From Eloise Wilkin's Book of Poems *by Deborah Wilkin Springett*

At Sunset

From Grandma's house we're homeward bound
As dusk begins its evening round.

The snow that's fallen on our street
Makes crunching sounds beneath our feet.

The sky glows red at close of day—
We marvel at the sun's display.

The sun sinks downward in the west
As horse and sleigh come home to rest,

And little footsteps in the snow
Trail homeward in the afterglow.

Eloise Burns Wilkin:
The Soul of Little Golden Books

A remembrance written by Jane Werner Watson in 1987

If you were to lay out a sampling of the thousand or so Little Golden Books that have been published during the past forty-five years and ask people who grew up with them, as millions of children did, which ones typified to them the essence of Little Golden Books, it is a fair guess that a majority would select those illustrated by Eloise Wilkin. When forty-eight titles were selected for inclusion in *The Treasury of Little Golden Books*, published in 1960, not surprisingly ten of them featured her work.

From the time the young Eloise descended upon New York with a portfolio almost as big as she was, until very recently, she was happily occupied illustrating books for children. Her work, she said, was "in her bones." Certainly it came also straight from her at once wise and innocent heart. What she shared with children—and their parents and grand-parents—was in fact her world and her life.

The mother of four children, she drew—and painted—the chubby, wide-eyed, eager but well-behaved toddlers every parent-to-be dreams of having. A lifetime resident of the Finger Lakes region of upper New York State, as an artist she placed her youngsters in idyllic rural settings with birds' nests in every branching tree—look, don't touch!—as well as daisies in the meadows for the picking, scampering squirrels, shy bunnies, unpolluted brooks in which to wade, and hip-roofed red barns in neat farmyards behind solid homes of fieldstone or white clapboard around which the colorful seasons turned.

A warm and creative homemaker, Eloise shared with the world glimpses of her big, busy, welcoming household, its rooms papered with gentle patterns, its drop-leaf tables and rocking chairs aglow with hand-rubbed sheen, its four-poster beds covered by hand-stitched quilts. A devoutly religious person, she shared ever so gently her values, her sense of the beauty of order and love, of implicit self-discipline, and of regard for others. In her voluminous work she has left us, only slightly idealized, rich reminders of a lovely time not very long ago.